*Railway Series, No*

# DUCK AND THE D

by
THE REV. W. A

with illustrations by
JOHN T. KENNEY

**KAYE & WARD LIMITED**
21 NEW STREET, LONDON EC2M 4NT

*First published by Edmund Ward (Publishers) Ltd 1958*
*Reprinted 1965*
*Reprinted by Kaye & Ward Ltd*
*21 New Street, London EC2M 4NT*
*1968, 1975*
*First printed in paperback form 1975*

ISBN 0 7182 0012 8 *(hardback)*
ISBN 0 7182 0437 9 *(paperback)*

*Printed in Great Britain by Tinling (1973) Limited, Prescot, Merseyside*
*A member of the Oxley Printing Group*

DEAR FRIENDS,

We have had two visitors to Our Railway. One of these, "City of Truro", is a very famous engine. We were sorry when we had to say "goodbye" to him.

The other visitor was different. "I do not believe," writes the Fat Controller, "that all Diesels are troublesome; but this one upset our engines, and made Duck very unhappy."

THE AUTHOR

# Domeless Engines

A SPECIAL train arrived one day, and the Fat Controller welcomed the passengers. They looked at everything in the Yard, and photographed the engines. Duck's Driver let some of them ride in his cab.

"They're the Railway Society," his Driver explained. "They've come to see us. Their engine's 'City of Truro'. He was the first to go 100 miles an hour. Let's get finished, then we can go and talk to him."

"Oh!" said Duck, awed. "He's too famous to notice me."

"Rubbish!" smiled his Driver. "Come on."

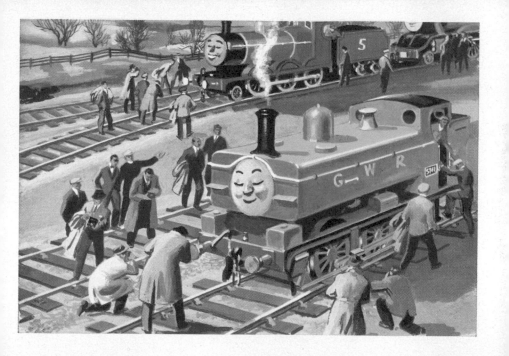

Duck found "City of Truro" at the coaling stage.

"May I talk to you?" he asked shyly.

"Of course," smiled the famous engine, "I see you are one of Us."

"I try to teach them Our ways," said Duck modestly.

"All ship-shape and Swindon fashion. That's right."

"Please, could you tell me how you beat the South Western?"

So "City of Truro" told Duck all about his famous run from Plymouth to Bristol more than fifty years ago. They were soon firm friends, and talked "Great Western" till late at night.

"City of Truro" left early next morning.

"Good riddance!" grumbled Gordon. "Chattering all night keeping important engines awake! Who *is* he anyway?"

"He's 'City of Truro'. He's famous."

"As famous as me? Nonsense!"

"He's famouser than you. He went 100 miles an hour before you were drawn or thought of."

"So he says; but I didn't like his looks. *He's got no dome*," said Gordon darkly. "Never trust domeless engines, they're not respectable.

"I never boast," Gordon continued modestly; "but 100 miles an hour would be easy for me. Goodbye!"

8

Presently Duck took some trucks to Edward's station. He was cross, and it was lucky for those trucks that they tried no tricks.

"Hullo!" called Edward. "The famous 'City of Truro' came through this morning. He whistled to me; wasn't he kind?"

"He's the finest engine in the world," said Duck, and he told Edward about "City of Truro", and what Gordon had said.

"Don't take any notice," soothed Edward, "he's just jealous. He thinks no engine should be famous but him. Look! He's coming now."

Gordon's boiler seemed to have swollen larger than ever. He was running very fast. He swayed up and down and from side to side as his wheels pounded the rails.

"He did it! I'll do it! He did it! I'll do it!" he panted. His train rocketed past and was gone.

Edward chuckled and winked at Duck. "Gordon's trying to do a 'City of Truro'," he said.

Duck was still cross. "I should think he'll knock himself to bits," he snorted. "I heard something rattle as he went through."

Gordon's Driver eased him off. "Steady boy!" he said. "We aren't running a race."

"We are then," said Gordon; but he said it to himself.

"I've never known him ride so roughly before," remarked his Driver.

His Fireman grabbed the brake handle to steady himself. "He's giving himself a hammering, and no mistake."

Soon Gordon began to feel a little queer. "The top of my boiler seems funny," he thought; "it's just as if something was loose. I'd better go slower."

But by then it was too late!

They met the wind on the viaduct. It wasn't ust a gentle wind; nor was it a hard steady wind. It was a teasing wind which blew suddenly in hard puffs, and caught you unawares.

Gordon thought it wanted to push him off the bridge. "No you don't!" he said firmly.

But the wind had other ideas. It curled round his boiler, crept under his loose dome, and lifted it off and away into the valley below. It fell on the rocks with a clang.

Gordon was most uncomfortable. He felt cold where his dome wasn't, and besides, people laughed at him as he passed.

At the Big Station, he tried to "Wheeeesh" them away; but they crowded round no matter what he did.

On the way back, he wanted his driver to stop and find his dome, and was very cross when he wouldn't.

He hoped the shed would be empty; but all the engines were there waiting.

"Never trust domeless engines," said a voice. "They aren't respectable."

# Pop Goes the Diesel

"CITY OF TRURO'S" visit made Duck very proud of being Great Western. He talked endlessly about it. But he worked hard too and made everything go like clockwork.

The trucks behaved well, the coaches were ready on time, and the passengers even stopped grumbling!

But the engines didn't like having to bustle about. "There are two ways of doing things," Duck told them, "the Great Western way, or the wrong way. I'm Great Western and . . ."

"Don't we know it!" they groaned. They were glad when a visitor came.

The visitor purred smoothly towards them. The Fat Controller climbed down. "Here is Diesel," he said, "I have agreed to give him a trial. He needs to learn. Please teach him, Duck."

"Good morning," purred Diesel in an oily voice, "pleased to meet you, Duck. Is that James?—*and* Henry?—*and* Gordon too? I am delighted to meet such famous engines." And he purred towards them.

The silly engines were flattered. "He has very good manners," they murmured, "we are pleased to have him in our Yard."

Duck had his doubts.

"Come on!" he said shortly.

"Ah! yes!" said Diesel, "The Yard, of course. Excuse me, engines," and he purred after Duck, talking hard. "Your worthy Fat . . ."

"Sir Topham Hatt to you," ordered Duck.

Diesel looked hurt. "Your worthy Sir Topham Hatt thinks I need to learn. He is mistaken. We Diesels don't need to learn. We know everything. We come to a yard and improve it. We are revolutionary."

"Oh!" said Duck, "If you're revo-thingummy, perhaps you would collect my trucks, while I fetch Gordon's coaches."

Diesel, delighted to show off, purred away. With much banging and clashing he collected a row of trucks. Duck left Gordon's coaches in the Station and came back.

Diesel was now trying to take some trucks from a siding nearby. They were old and empty. Clearly they had not been touched for a long time.

Their brakes would not come off properly. Diesel found them hard to move.

Pull—Push—Backwards—Forwards. "Oheeeer! Oheeeer!" the trucks groaned. "We can't! We *won't!*"

Duck watched the operation with interest.

Diesel lost patience. "GrrrrrRRRRRrrrrr-RRRRR!" he roared, and gave a great heave. The trucks jerked forward.

"Oher! Oher!" they screamed. "We *can't!* We *WON'T!*" Some of their brakes broke, and the gear hanging down bumped on the rails and sleepers.

"WE CAN'T! WE WON'T! Aaaah!" Their trailing brakes caught in the points and locked themselves solid.

"GrrrrrRRRRRrrrrrRRRRRrrrrrRRRR!" roared Diesel; a rusty coupling broke, and he shot forward suddenly by himself.

"Ho! Ho! Ho!" chuckled Duck.

Diesel recovered and tried to push the trucks back; but they wouldn't move, and he had to give up. Duck ran quietly round to where the other trucks all stood in line. "Thank you for arranging these, Diesel," he said, "I must go now."

"Don't you want this lot?"

"No thank you."

Diesel gulped. "And I've taken all this trouble," he almost shrieked. "Why didn't you tell me?"

"You never asked me. Besides," said Duck innocently, "you were having such fun being revo-whatever-it-was-you-said. Goodbye."

Diesel had to help the workmen clear the mess. He hated it. All the trucks and coaches were laughing. Presently he heard them singing. Their song grew louder and louder, and soon it echoed through the Yard.

Trucks are waiting in the Yard; tackling them with
          ease'll
"Show the world what I can do," gaily boasts the Diesel.
In and out he creeps about, like a big black weasel.
When he pulls the wrong trucks out—Pop goes the
          Diesel!

"Grrrrr!" he growled, and scuttling away, sulked in the Shed.

# Dirty Work

WHEN Duck returned, and heard the trucks singing, he was horrified. "Shut up!" he ordered, and bumped them hard. "I'm sorry our trucks were rude to you, Diesel," he said.

Diesel was still furious. "It's all your fault. You made them laugh at me," he complained.

"Nonsense," said Henry, "Duck would never do that. We engines have our differences; but we *never* talk about them to trucks. That would be des—des . . ."

"Disgraceful!" said Gordon.

"Disgusting!" put in James.

"Despicable!" finished Henry.

Diesel hated Duck. He wanted him to be sent away. So he made a plan.

Next day he spoke to the trucks. "I see you like jokes," he said in his oily voice. "You made a good joke about me yesterday. I laughed and laughed. Duck told me one about Gordon. I'll whisper it. . . . Don't tell Gordon I told you," and he sniggered away.

"Haw! haw! haw!" guffawed the trucks. "Gordon will be cross with Duck when he knows. Let's tell him and pay Duck out for bumping us."

Diesel went to all the sidings, and in each he told different stories. He said Duck had told them to him. This was untrue; but the trucks didn't know.

They laughed rudely at the engines as they went by, and soon Gordon, Henry and James found out why.

"Disgraceful!" said Gordon.

"Disgusting!" said James.

"Despicable!" said Henry. "We cannot allow it."

They consulted together. "Yes," they said, "he did it to us. We'll do it to him, and see how *he* likes it."

Duck was tired out. The trucks had been cheeky and troublesome. He had had hard work to make them behave. He wanted a rest in the Shed.

"Hoooooooosh! KEEP OUT!" The three engines barred his way, and Diesel lurked behind.

"Stop fooling," said Duck, "I'm tired."

"So are we," hissed the engines. "We are tired of *you*. We like Diesel. We don't like you. You tell tales about us to trucks."

"I don't."

"You do."

"I don't."

"You do."

The Fat Controller came to stop the noise.

"Duck called me a 'galloping sausage'," spluttered Gordon.

". . . rusty red scrap-iron," hissed James.

". . . I'm 'old square wheels'," fumed Henry.

"Well Duck?"

Duck considered. "I only wish Sir," he said gravely, "that I'd thought of those names myself. If the dome fits . . ."

"Ha! Ahem!" The Fat Controller coughed.

"He made trucks laugh at us," accused the engines.

The Fat Controller recovered. "Did you, Duck?"

"Certainly not Sir! No *steam* engine would be as mean as that."

"Now Diesel, you heard what Duck said."

"I can't understand it Sir. To think that Duck of all engines . . . I'm dreadfully grieved Sir; but know nothing."

"I see." Diesel squirmed and hoped he didn't.

"I am sorry, Duck," the Fat Controller went on; "but you must go to Edward's station for a while. I know he will be glad to see you."

"Beg pardon Sir, do you mean now?"

"Yes please."

"As you wish Sir." Duck trundled sadly away, while Diesel smirked with triumph in the darkness.

## A Close Shave

So Duck came to Edward's station.

"It's not fair," he complained, "Diesel has made the Fat Controller and all the engines think I'm horrid."

Edward smiled. "I know you aren't," he said, "and so does the Fat Controller. You wait and see."

Duck felt happier with Edward. He helped him with his trucks and coaches, and sometimes helped foreign engines by pushing their trains up the hill.

But Gordon, Henry and James never spoke to him at all.

One day he pushed behind a goods train and helped it to the top.

"Peep peep! Goodbye!" he called, and rolled gently over the crossing to the other line. Duck loved coasting down the hill, running easily with the wind whistling past. He hummed a little tune.

----

"Peeeeeep! Peeeeeep! Peeeeeeep!"

"That sounds like a Guard's whistle," he thought. "But we haven't a Guard."

His Driver heard it too, and looked back. "Hurry, Duck, hurry," he called urgently. "There's been a break-away, some trucks are chasing us."

There were twenty heavily loaded trucks. "Hurrah! Hurrah! Hurrah!" they laughed, "We've broken away! We've broken away! We've broken away!" and before the signalman could change the points they followed Duck on to the down line.

"Chase him! Bump him! Throw him off the rails!" they yelled, and hurtled after Duck, bumping and swaying with ever-increasing speed.

The Guard saved Duck. Though the trucks had knocked him off his van, he got up and ran behind, blowing his whistle to attract the Driver's attention.

"Now what?" asked the Fireman.

"As fast as we can," said the Driver grimly, "then they'll catch us gradually."

They raced through Edward's station whistling furiously, but the trucks caught them with a shuddering jar. The Fireman climbed back, and the van brakes came on with a scream.

Braking carefully, the Driver was gaining control.

"Another clear mile and we'll do it," he said.

They swept round a bend.

"Oh glory! look at that!"

A passenger train was just pulling out on their line, from the station ahead.

The Driver leapt to his reverser; Hard over —Full steam—Whistle.

"It's up to you now, Duck," he said.

Duck put every ounce of weight and steam against the trucks.

They felt his strength. "On! On!" they yelled; but Duck was holding them now.

"I must stop them. I *must*."

The station came nearer and nearer. The last coach cleared the platform.

"It's too late," Duck groaned, and shut his eyes.

He felt a sudden swerve, and slid, shuddering and groaning along a siding.

A barber had set up shop in a wooden shed in the yard. He was shaving a customer.

There was a sliding groaning crash, and part of the wall caved in.

The customer jumped nervously; but the barber held him down. "It's only an engine," he said calmly, and went on lathering.

"Beg pardon Sir!" gasped Duck, "Excuse my intrusion."

"No. I won't," said the barber crossly, "you've frightened my customers and spoilt my new paint. I'll teach you." And he lathered Duck's face all over.

Poor Duck.

They were pulling the trucks away when the Fat Controller arrived. The Barber was telling the workmen what he thought.

"I do *not* like engines popping through my walls," he fumed. "They disturb my customers."

"I appreciate your feelings," said the Fat Controller, "and we'll gladly repair the damage; but you must know that this engine and his crew have prevented a serious accident. You and many others might have been badly hurt."

The Fat Controller paused impressively. "It was a very close shave," he said.

"Oh!" said the barber, "Oh! Excuse me."
He ran into his shop, fetched a basin of water,
and washed Duck's face.

"I'm sorry, Duck," he said. "I didn't know
you were being a brave engine."

"That's all right, Sir," said Duck. "I didn't
know that either."

"You were very brave indeed," said the Fat
Controller kindly. "I'm proud of you. I shall
tell 'City of Truro' about you next time he
comes."

"Oh Sir!" Duck felt happier than he had
been for weeks.

"And now," said the Fat Controller, "when you are mended you are coming home."

"Home Sir? Do you mean the Yard?"

"Of course."

"But Sir, they don't like me. They like Diesel."

"Not now." The Fat Controller smiled. "I never believed Diesel. After you went he told lies about Henry; so I sent him packing. The engines are sorry and want you back."

So, when a few days later he came home shining with new paint, there was a really rousing welcome for Duck the Great Western engine.